How Many Feet In The Bed?

How Many Feet In The Bed?

by Diane Johnston Hamm

illustrated by Kate Salley Palmer

Simon & Schuster Books for Young Readers

PUBLISHED BY SIMON & SCHUSTER

New York · London · Toronto · Sydney · Tokyo · Singapore

SIMON & SCHUSTER BOOKS FOR YOUNG READERS
Simon & Schuster Building, Rockefeller Center,
1230 Avenue of the Americas, New York, New York 10020.
Text copyright © 1991 by Diane Johnston Hamm.
Illustrations copyright © 1991 by Kate Salley Palmer.

SIMON & SCHUSTER BOOKS FOR YOUNG READERS
is a trademark of Simon & Schuster
Designed by Lucille Chomowicz
Manufactured in Singapore
1   3   5   7   9   8   6   4   2
LIBRARY OF CONGRESS CATALOGING-IN-PUBLICATION DATA
Hamm, Diane Johnston.
How many feet in the bed? Summary: Count the feet as a family of five tumble in and out of
bed on a Sunday morning.
[1. Bedtime—Fiction.   2. Family life—Fiction.   3. Counting.]
I. Palmer, Kate Salley, ill.   II. Title.
[E]—dc20   90-35724
ISBN 0-671-72638-2

To the feet in my bed —DJH

To Merv, for the enlightenment, and to Jim, for everything —KSP

When my father wakes up, I ask him, "How many feet are in the bed?"

He says, "I thought there were two."

Not now!
With me here,
I see four!

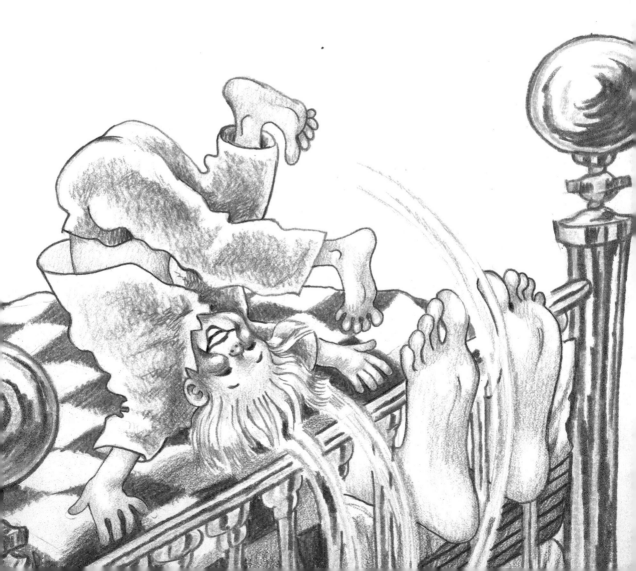

One, two, three, four.
Four feet in the bed.
Tom's feet smell.
Don't let him in!

Uh-oh. Now there are six!
One, two, three, four, five, six.
Six feet in the bed.

"Look again," says Mom.
"With Baby Jane, you now have eight!"
One, two, three, four, five, six, seven, eight.

Eight feet in the bed.
Dad says, "If Mom will
join us, we'll have ten!"

One, two, three, four, five, six,
seven, eight, nine, ten.

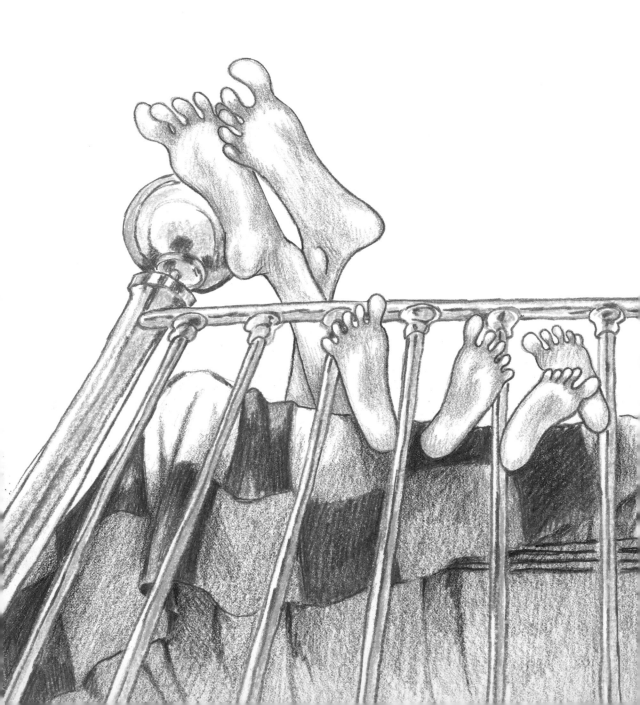

Ten feet in the bed.

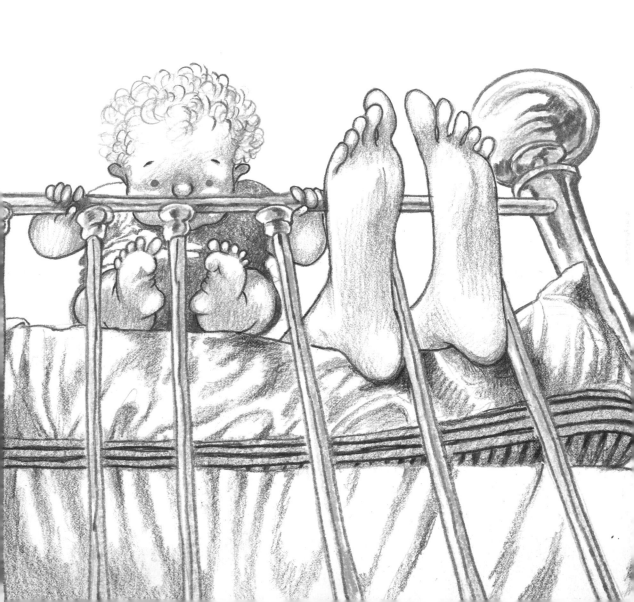

Two feet, four feet,
six, eight, ten.
We're all comfy in our
warm little nest.

B-r-r-ring!
There goes the phone.

Dad jumps up to answer.
Now there are eight feet
in the bed.

Splash! Water spills over the tub.
Mom leaves in a hurry.
Now there are six feet in the bed.

Yikes! It's cartoon time.
"So long, Tom."
There are four feet in the bed.

"Mom! The baby is wet!
Bye-bye, Jane."
Now there are only two feet left.

But not for long—
I smell breakfast....

There are no feet left in the bed.
There is just—

—one sleepy bear
instead.